MY
BEDTIME RHY

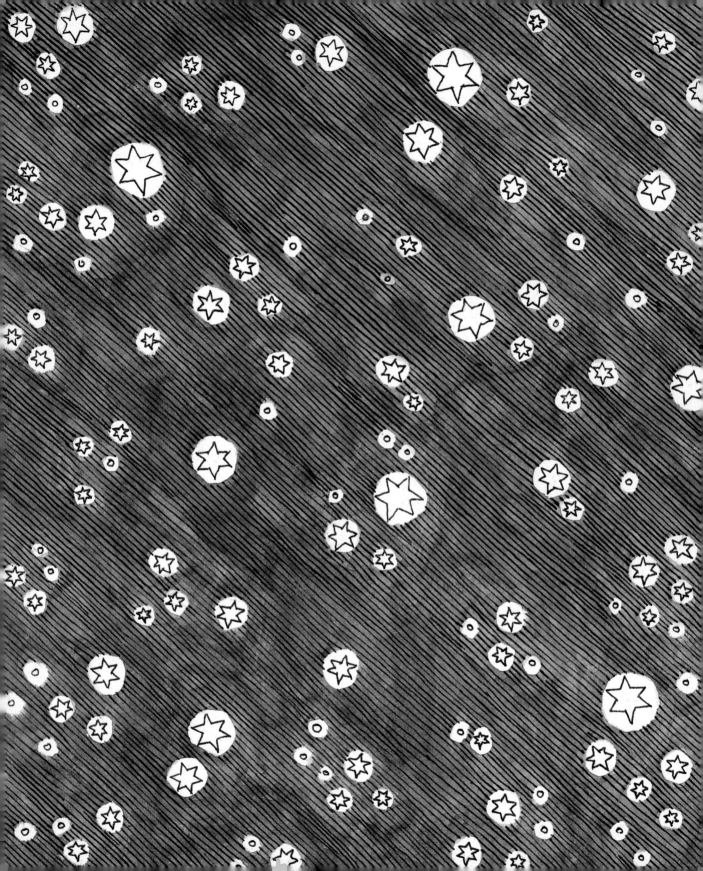

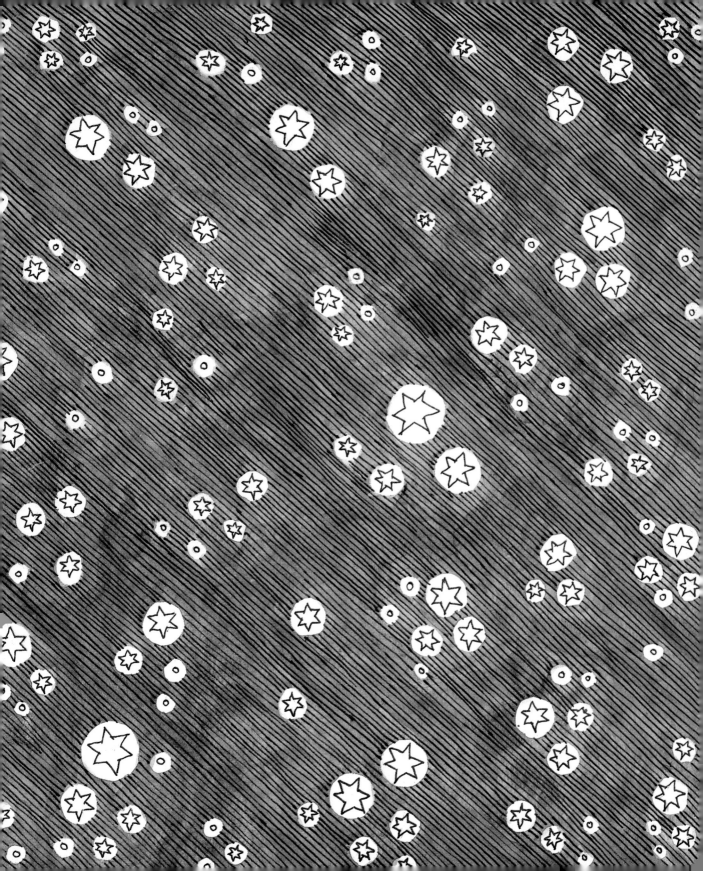

To my parents,
and for Rosy

A Beaver Book
Published by Arrow Books Limited
62-65 Chandos Place, London WC2N 4NW
An imprint of Century Hutchinson Ltd

London Melbourne Sydney Auckland
Johannesburg and agencies throughout the world

First published in Great Britain by Andersen Press 1987

Beaver edition 1988

Printed and bound in Italy by Grafiche AZ, Verona

ISBN 0 09 954790 2

MY
BEDTIME RHYME

Jane Johnson

Beaver Books

One night I lay in bed
And couldn't go to sleep.
I watched the moonlight moving
Making monster shadows creep.

I hid beneath the bedclothes
And the sheets shut out the light.

When I opened up my eyes again...

The whole world was all white!

I rushed around a reindeer
And then raced out of reach.

I jumped into a basket

And ballooned above a beach.

I nodded to a nestling

And it nipped me on the nose.

I dropped onto a donkey...

And disturbed it from its doze.

I fell among some hissing snakes.

A tiger snarled at me.

I thought I heard a crocodile
And stood up to try and see.

I kept my eyes wide open.
I didn't run and hide.

Then I met a mad old magpie,

Chased the moon

with all my might

And woke up in broad daylight!

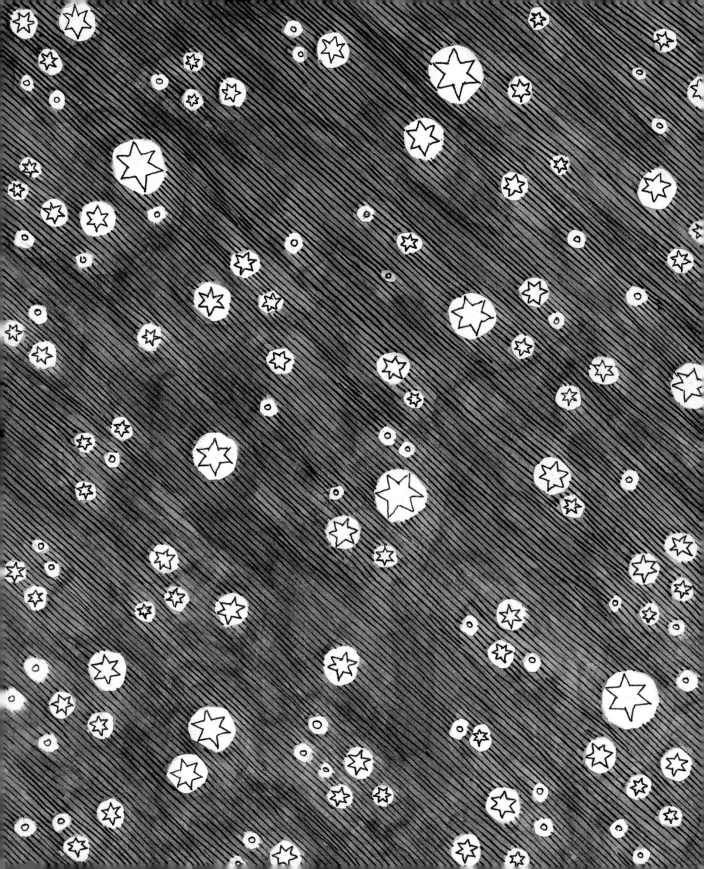

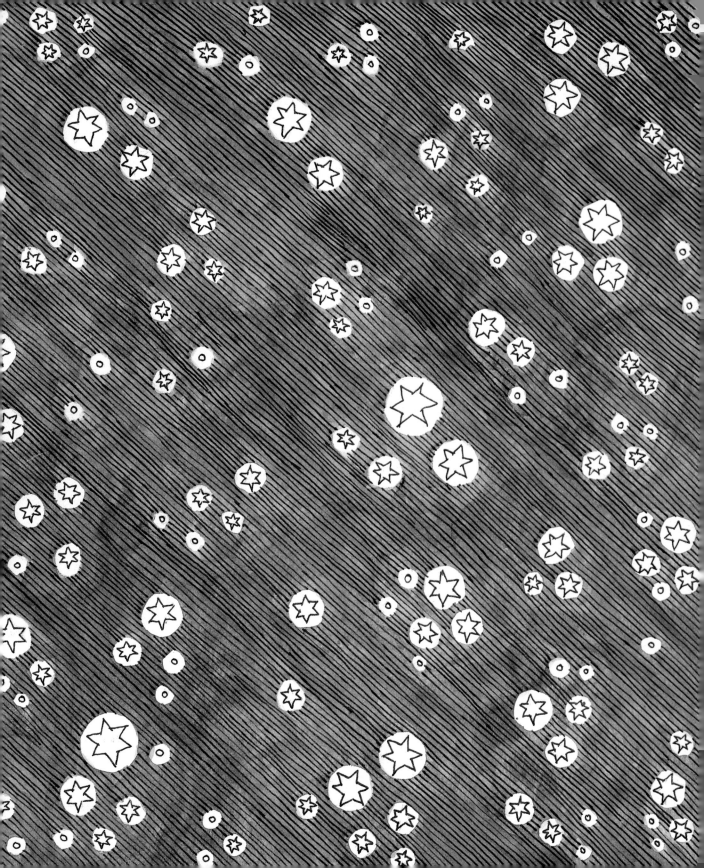